Steven the Vegan

Written by Dan Bodenstein

Illustrated by Ron Robrahn

Totem Tales Publishing, LLC

web: www.totemtales.com
email: books@totemtales.com

Phone: (561) 537-2522

First published by Totem Tales Publishing 07/21/2012

ISBN: 978-0-9843228-9-3

Printed in the United States of America

For information on sales and distribution, please contact:

Totem Tales Publishing LLC
(561) 537-2522
books@totemtales.com

For my wife Cindy, for being my inspiration, and an inspiration to others to treat all animals better than we treat ourselves.

Special Thanks To :

David & Gloria Hamilton
Lettie Harrald
Casey Libourel
Tracy's Cheesecakes, Buffalo Vegetarian Society
Stephen (the Vegan) Kowarsky
Elizabeth Gonsalves
Cindy Taffel

Visit StevenTheVegan.com to learn more.

vegan [ˈviːgən]

a person who doesn't use animal products for food, clothing, or any other purpose.

A farm sanctuary is a special farm where animals can run, play, and live their lives in happiness.

The farm was far away from the city where Steven went to school. By the time the students arrived, it was time to have lunch.

Marion noticed that Steven's lunch was a peanut butter and jelly sandwich, and he also had some carrots, and celery.

"Eeew," she said. "Steven's eating vegetables."

The other children looked at Steven, who was quietly eating his sandwich. "Why do you eat vegetables?" asked Rusty, the red-haired boy.

"Why?" asked Marion.

"Because animals are my friends,
    not my food," said Steven.

"What do you mean?" she asked.

"Come with me." said Steven. " I'll show you."

Steven and his classmates walked over to the fenced area where the cows were grazing in the pasture.

One of the cows came over to the fence, and Steven climbed onto the fence. "Cows are gentle animals," explained Steven.

"I don't eat cows," said Marion.

"Do you eat hamburgers?" asked Steven. "Hamburger comes from cows."

"Eeew," cried Marion.

"You know what else comes from cows?"
"Milk!" shouted Andrea.
"Right," said Steven. "Cows make milk to feed baby cows. It takes thousands of cows to make all the milk people drink."

Marion and her classmate Andrea knelt down to pet the baby calves.

"I don't want to take milk away from this little guy." said Andrea.

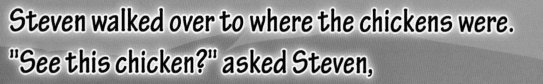

Steven walked over to where the chickens were.
"See this chicken?" asked Steven,
"This is where your chicken nuggets, chicken wings and
fried chicken comes from."

"Which part is the nugget?" asked Andrea.

Steven just shrugged his shoulders. He didn't know what part of the chicken the nugget came from.

"Everyone knows chickens lay eggs," said Steven. "But did you know that if we didn't eat eggs, then those eggs would hatch little baby chicks?"

Steven took his classmates over to the pig pen.

Inside, several pigs were rolling around and playing in the mud.

"Do you eat bacon, ham, or pork chops?" asked Steven. Marion nodded her head "Yes." "Well all those come from pigs. If they eat slop and you eat them, then you're eating their slop too. Remember, you are what you eat."

"I didn't know bacon was pig," said Dwayne, petting the little pig. "I thought bacon was just -- um --. bacon."
"Well, I didn't know that either," said Andrea. "I'm not eating bacon or anything else that comes from these cute little piggies."

Steven and his friends headed over to the barn. On the way they came upon some fluffy sheep.

He looked at his classmates, "Anyone want lamb chops?" Nobody answered him. "Lamb chops come from baby sheep." He patted the little lamb on the head.

Steven and his classmates walked into the big red barn. Inside were many horses, and an old farm dog.

As they entered the barn, Rusty said, "Don't tell me horseradish comes from horses?"

Steven laughed. "No. But if you wouldn't eat a horse, why would you eat a cow?"

"Just because I don't eat meat doesn't mean I just eat salads. I eat rice, pasta, even veggie burgers with French fries."

"But how can I grow up to be big and strong like my dad just by eating vegetables? Don't I need milk and meat for that?" asked Andy.

"How many of you like dinosaurs?" asked Steven.
All his friends raised their hands.

"Many dinosaurs were vegans. Like the Brachiosaurus, Stegosaurus, and Triceratops.

"They only ate leaves, grasses, and other plants, and they were some of the largest animals that roamed the Earth." "Yeah, but all of them are extinct," said Marion.

"But there are other animals that we all know of that are vegan," explained Steven. "Like what?" asked Marion.

"Like hippos, elephants, rhinos, giraffes, buffalo, and gorillas," explained Steven.
"I love giraffes.", shouted Marion.

As they walked back to the picnic table area, Dwayne said, "Well, I'm telling my mom and dad that I'm not eating animals anymore. Animals are my friends, not food."

Most of all, he was glad just knowing how many cows, chickens, pigs, and other animals might be saved. Those animals could grow up and live full, fun lives, just like him and his classmates.

48914010R00023